I

FE

The Piggy in the Puddle

The Piggy in the Puddle

Words by CHARLOTTE POMERANTZ
Pictures by JAMES MARSHALL

MACMILLAN PUBLISHING COMPANY
New York

Macmillan Publishing Company, 866 Third Avenue, New York, N.Y. 10022
Collier Macmillan Canada, Inc.
Library of Congress catalog card number: 73-6047
Printed in the United States of America
7 8 9 10 11 12 13

The illustrations were prepared as pen and ink drawings, with halftone overlays for brown, green, yellow and pink. The typeface is Alphatype Aster, and the display is hand-lettered by the artist.

Library of Congress Cataloging in Publication Data
Pomerantz, Charlotte. The piggy in the puddle. [1. Stories in rhyme]
I. Marshall, James, date illus. II. Title
PZ8.3.P564Pi [E] 73-6047 ISBN 0-02-774900-2

For Gabrielle, Daniel and Jennifer — C. P.

For Eloise Clifton — J. M.

See the piggy,
See the puddle,
See the muddy little puddle.
See the piggy in the middle
Of the muddy little puddle.
See her dawdle, see her diddle
In the muddy, muddy middle.
See her waddle, plump and little,
In the very merry middle.

See her daddy,
Fuddy-duddy, fuddy-duddy, fuddy-duddy.
"Don't you get all muddy,
Muddy, muddy, muddy, muddy.
You are much too plump and little
To be in the muddy middle.
Mud is squishy, mud is squashy,
Mud is oh so squishy-squashy.
What you need is lots of soap."
But the piggy answered,
"Squishy-squashy, squishy-squashy—NOPE!"

SOAP
dVOS
NOPe!

See her mommy,
Fiddle-faddle, fiddle-faddle, fiddle-faddle.
"Get out of there—skedaddle,
Daddle, daddle, daddle, daddle.
You are much too plump and little
To be in the muddy middle.
Mud is mooshy, mud is squooshy,
Mud is oh so mooshy-squooshy.
What you need is lots of soap."
But the piggy answered,
"Mooshy-squooshy, mooshy-squooshy—NOPE!"

SOAP
NOPe!

See her brother,
Silly billy, silly billy, silly billy.
"Do not waddle willy-nilly,
Willy-nilly, willy-nilly.
You are much too plump and little
To be in the muddy middle.
Mud is oofy, mud is poofy,
Mud is oh so oofy-poofy.
What you need is lots of soap."

But the piggy answered,
"Oofy-poofy, oofy-poofy—NOPE!"

NOPe!

Now they all stood in a huddle,
Right beside the muddy puddle.
And they looked into the puddle—
What a muddy, muddy muddle!

There was piggy, plump and little,
In the very merry middle.
She was waddling, she was paddling,
She was diving way down derry.
She was wiggling, she was giggling,
She was very, very merry.
Said the mother,
"Little piggy, you have made me very mad."
Said the father,
"Little piggy, you have made me very sad."
"Little piggy," said the brother,
"You are very, very bad."
Said the piggy,
"Squishy-squashy, mooshy-squooshy, very bad."

"Dear, oh dear," said piggy's mother.
"What's a mother pig to do?"
She thought and thought and thought and thought—
And then, of course, she knew.
She said, "I bet my feet get wet."
And — jumped — in — too!

See two piggies in the puddle,
In the muddy little puddle.
See the piggy and her mommy
In the muddy little puddle.
"Me oh my," said piggy's father.
"What's a father pig to do?"
He thought and thought and thought and thought—
And then, of course, he knew.
He said, "I bet my tail gets wet."
And — jumped — in — too!

See three piggies in the puddle,
In the muddy little puddle.
See mommy, daddy, piggy
In the muddy little puddle.
"Boo-hoo-hoo," cried piggy's brother.
"Whatever shall I do?"
He thought, but not for very long,
Because, of course, he knew.
He held his nose and yelled, "Here goes!"
And — jumped — in — too!

See four piggies in the puddle,
In the muddy little puddle.
See the piggies in the middle
Of the muddy little puddle.
See them diddle, big and little,
In the very merry middle.
Said the daddy, "Mud is squishy,
Mud is oh so squishy-squashy."
Said the mommy, "Mud is mooshy,
Mud is oh so mooshy-squooshy."
Said the brother, "Mud is oofy,
Mud is oh so oofy-poofy."

CLYDE's
SOAP

Said the piggy,
"Squishy-squashy, mooshy-squooshy, oofy-poofy.
Indeed," said little piggy,
"I think we need some soap."
But the other piggies answered,
"Oofy-poofy—NOPE!"

NOPE!
SOAP

So they all dove way down derry,
And were very, very merry.

SOAP